Dogs in Space ™

The Great Space Doghouse

Written and Illustrated by Nancy Coffelt

Dogs in Space™/by Nancy Coffelt

Library of Congress Control Number: 00-133106

Summary: Learn about the construction and the
day-to-day activities aboard Earth's real-life space
clubhouse, the International Space Station.

ISBN 1-883772-53-2

Printed in Mexico

This book was created with the cooperation of NASA's Johnson Space Center.
Special thanks to Gregory Vogt, Ed.D., of the University of Oklahoma for working
closely with NASA, Flying Rhinoceros, and Nancy Coffelt Studios.

For Al Richmond,
who has dedicated himself to space
science education.

Ursa Major loves science. With the help of Kirk and Dr. MIP, she is working on new and exciting projects.

Countdown, Sunspot, Luna, Zip, and Scotty love working on new things too. But they do not like working on this project. Ursa Major has them vacuuming!

Dogs in Space have been cleaning the laboratory all day.
What they really want to work on is a clubhouse. "Not in my
backyard," says Ursa Major. "You have three of them started
already. So, when you are done with your chores, you need

to find someplace else to build." The dogs have no idea where to start. "Well," says Mark, "the Earth is huge. I bet you can find a lot of places to build your clubhouse."

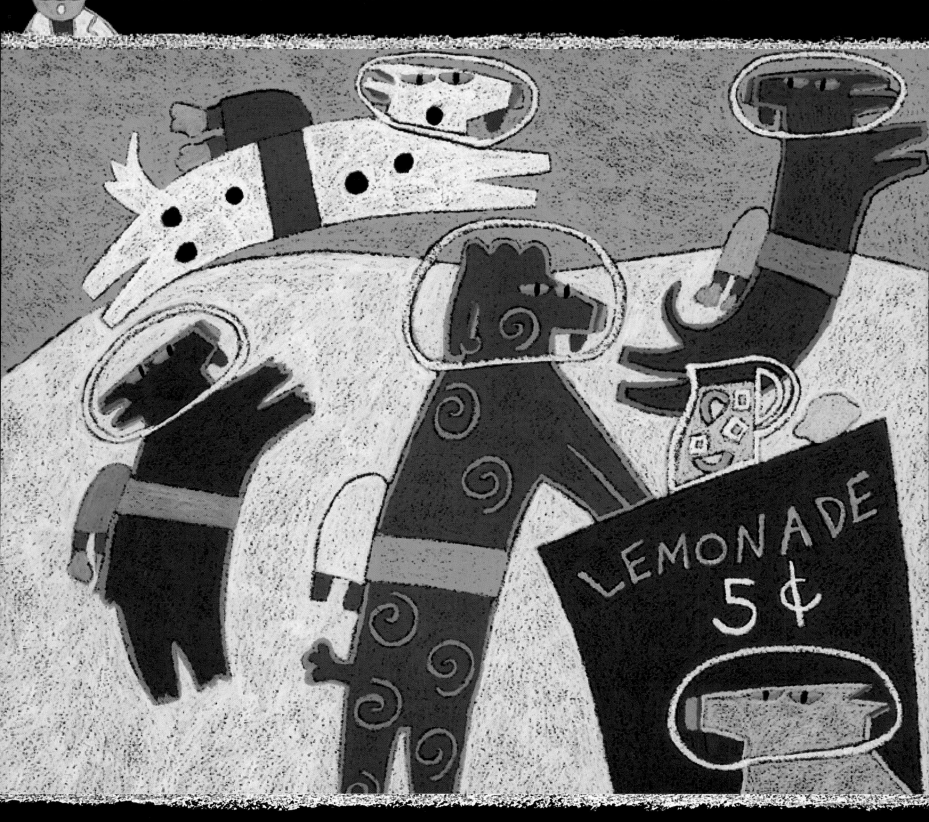

Zip wants to try someplace warm. Dogs in Space fly to the hottest desert. Luna opens a lemonade stand. The rest of them just pant.

Dogs in Space zoom to the coldest place they can find.
Scotty makes snow angels, but the rest of them just shiver.

Dogs in Space search high. Countdown practices his

Dogs in Space search low. They plunge to the depths of the ocean and dodge hammerhead sharks. But they can't agree on the perfect spot to build their clubhouse.

Dogs in Space have been all over the Earth. How about space?

A GREAT SPACE DOGHOUSE – the clubhouse just for Dogs in Space

The dogs have a lot of planning and work to do. Zip stands guard as strange sounds come from their top-secret workshop.

It takes a huge amount of energy for a rocket to blast off. The rocket has to fight Earth's gravity. (The Earth pulls objects towards it. This is called gravity.) Two rocket boosters are used to launch the space shuttle. These rockets are 149 feet long and 12 feet across.

Finally, all the pieces are loaded onto a rocket ship for the big blast-off into orbit.

Each weighs 1,300,000 pounds. When the shuttle is 150,000 feet up in the air, the rocket boosters stop working and fall into the ocean. Then people can find and use them again.

Dogs in Space zoom after the rocket ship to put their space doghouse together.

The International Space Station has 100 major parts and millions of little parts. People use regular tools like screwdrivers, pliers, and wrenches to put the space station together, but they also use special tools like jetpacks. Jetpacks are personal rockets.

There are many, many pieces to put together, but working in space is fun.

Astronauts wear jetpacks on their backpacks when they go outside the space station on a space walk. If they start to float away, they can use the jetpack's joystick to move back to the station.

Dogs in Space speed around with their jetpacks while building their clubhouse together. They use a lot of tools and a lot of teamwork.

The Great Space Doghouse is complete! The dogs love it! Sunspot looks out the window and counts the stars. Luna looks out the window and searches for aliens.

It will be like a delivery truck. The space shuttle will also be like a bus. It will take crewmembers back and forth between Earth and the station.

All the Dogs in Space look out the window and see the Earth.

The Great Space Doghouse has many of the same things we have on Earth. There is air to breathe. Dogs in Space need air. There is food to eat. Dogs in Space need food too.

The air will be heated to normal room temperature. Food will be kept in plastic packages. They will have favorites like macaroni and cheese, hot dogs, punch, and chocolate pudding.

There is even a laboratory for experiments. Sunspot likes playing mad scientist in the space lab.

The Great Space Doghouse doesn't have the feeling of gravity. Dogs in Space love to float. Zip flips and Luna somersaults.

is the same feeling as dropping on a roller coaster or a fast elevator. The crewmembers will feel this because the space station is actually moving in an orbit around the Earth.

When it's time for sleep, Dogs in Space curl up and weightlessly snore.

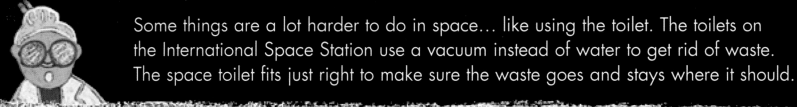

When they need it, the space doghouse has a special microgravity toilet.

And Ursa Major made sure that the Dogs in Space installed her Self-Contained-Outer-Space-Double-Bubble-Dog-Washer.

It is hard to take a shower in space. It takes a long time. A crewmember can only wash one small area of skin at a time. They use water from a small hose, soap up, and then wipe

Dogs in Space do not like baths. But Scotty wants to see what the dog washer is all about. It works just fine until Zip opens the door to the Self-Contained-Outer-Space-

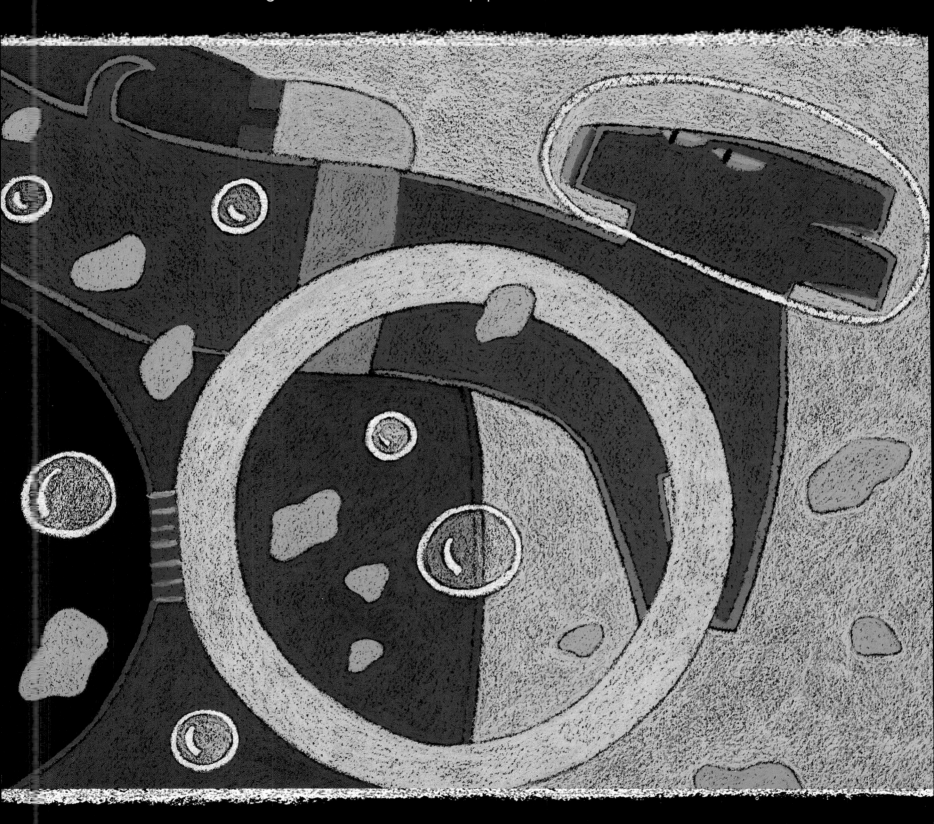

Double-Bubble-Dog-Washer to see what's inside. OH NO! Blobs of soapy water float out! Bubbles float out! A very soggy Scotty floats out!

The crew on the International Space Station has to keep the station very clean. They vacuum every day. It is important to keep dust, hair clippings, and other dirt out of the special science instruments.

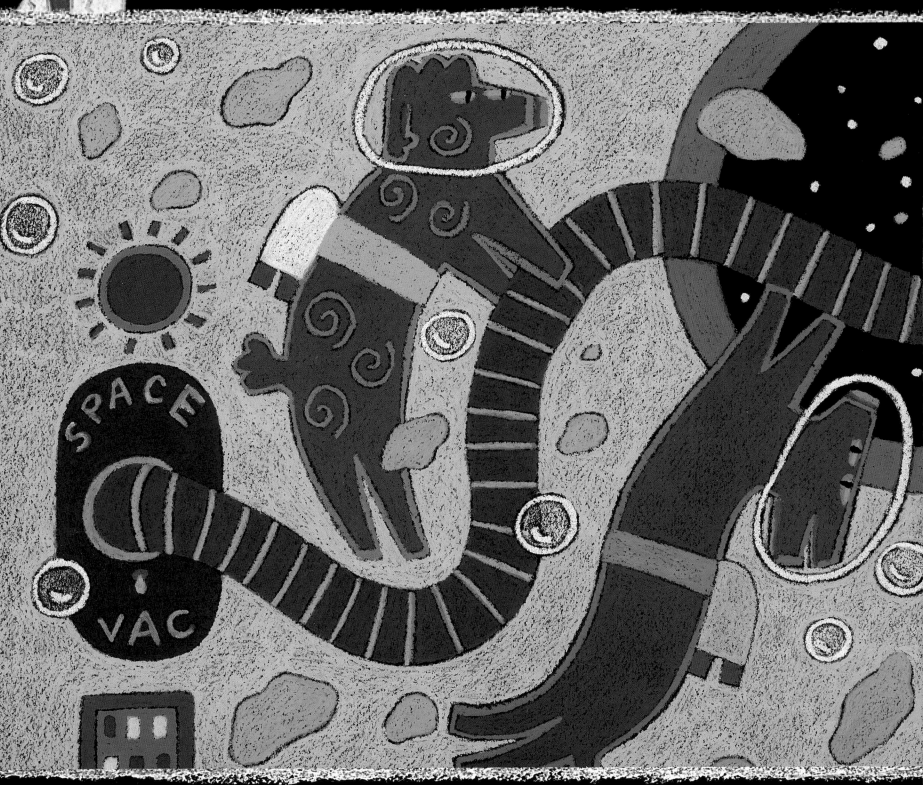

WHAT A MESS! Soapy water and bubbles are floating everywhere. Countdown grabs the space vacuum.

Dogs in Space take turns vacuuming up all the floating
soapy water and bubbles.

Every crewmember has chores. Cooking, answering e-mail, storing equipment, taking pictures, and putting in new parts brought by the space shuttle are just a few of the jobs in space.

Whew! Dogs in Space still have chores to do, even in space! Housecleaning is more fun with Ursa Major and Kirk. But Kirk and Ursa Major are back on Earth.

The roar of the sea, the feel of the wind, and the smell of freshly mown grass are back on Earth too. On Earth, there are swimming pools, movie popcorn, and big, open fields to run around and around in.

So Countdown, Sunspot, Luna, Zip, and Scotty zoom back to Earth.

"Nice to see you," says Ursa Major. "Glad you're back," says
Kirk. "Welcome home," says Dr. MIP. The Dogs in Space are
glad to be home, but they know they can always return to
their clubhouse in space – The Great Space Doghouse.